# Created by Chris Steward

## For my wife, my rock, my world.

For rights and permissions please contact Elora Publishing Limited — Land of Gonk
contact@landofgonk.co.uk

ISBN: 978-1-7391322-2-4
Printed in the UK by Lavenham Press, 47 Water Street, Lavenham, CO10 9RN
Illustrated by Sona & Jacob — www.sonaandjacob.com

Alf was looking forward to his holiday.
Having worked harder than most last
Christmas he was ready to have
a well earned break.

Unlike his last trip, he was even more
pleased to be taking his wife Alma and
his two children, Max and Ruby.

"Where are we going Daddy?"
asked Max.

"We are going to visit one of the most
AMAZING cities in the world..."

# LONDON

The children were excited to go to London
as it was their first trip on a plane. The family
arrived at the airport ready for the flight.

After their first night in London Alf and his family were eager to explore. However, when Alf read the morning paper, there was **bad** news.

THE GONK TIMES
TUBE STRIKES AND PROTESTS

"Oh no Dad, does this mean we'll have to walk everywhere?" grumbled Ruby.

"Don't worry children" said Alf. "I'm going to let you into a secret. Whilst London is famous for its underground trains, black taxis and red buses, there is a whole network of secret underground travel."

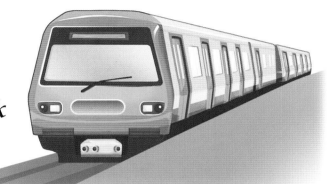

"We Gonks have kept the old tunnels and rivers alive and we'll be able to travel safely across London."

"But you must keep it secret. Humans do not know about it."

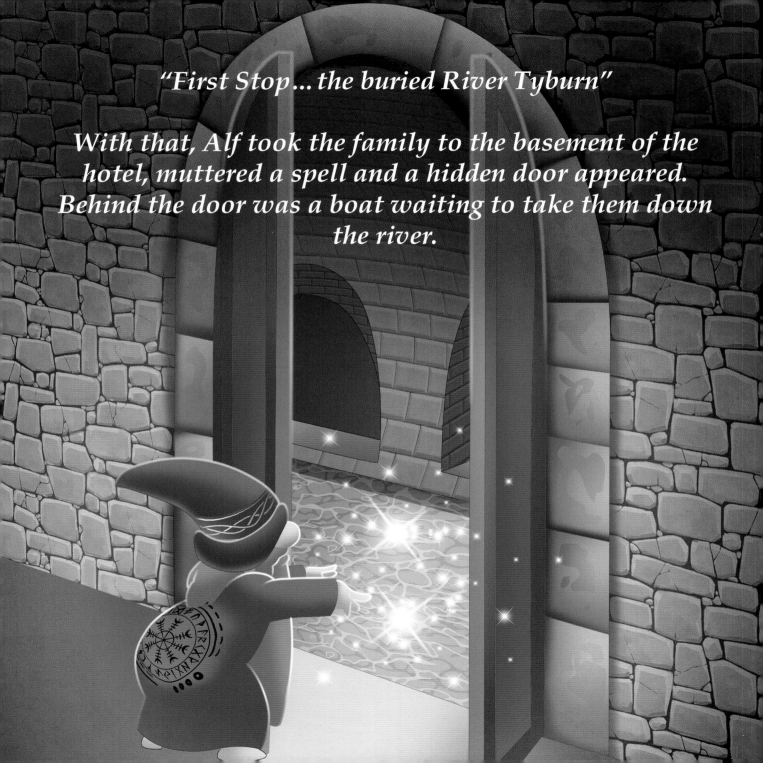

"First Stop... the buried River Tyburn"

With that, Alf took the family to the basement of the hotel, muttered a spell and a hidden door appeared. Behind the door was a boat waiting to take them down the river.

"To **Buckingham Palace**"
*shouted the children.*

*Buckingham Palace has been home to*
*The Kings and Queens of England for generations.*

*I bet you didn't know that The Royal Gonk*
*Family also live here protected by the*
*Royal Gonk Guards?*

*Next stop, The Houses of Parliament.*

*Taking another boat the family travelled under St James's Park to a chamber beneath Parliament.*

*"This vault is the hidden gateway for Gonks to get into Parliament."*

*"Now, on to the House of Commons!" said Alf.*

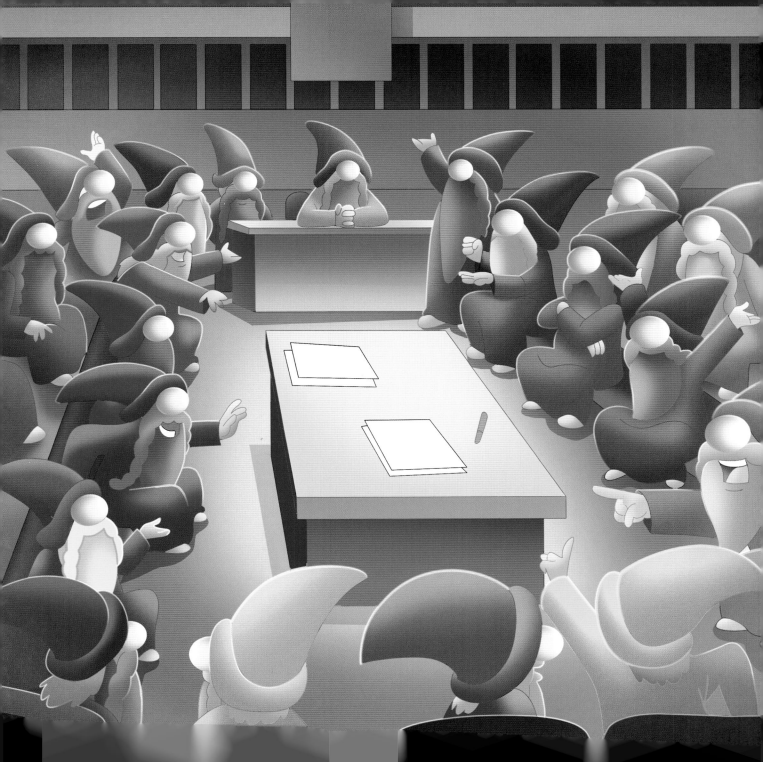

The debating chamber was very noisy so Max and Ruby were more than happy to continue their tour through Parliament.

The old heating system provided the perfect walkway through the palace allowing the Gonks to look into every room as they went.

"Maybe it would be better not to see this room" said Alf...

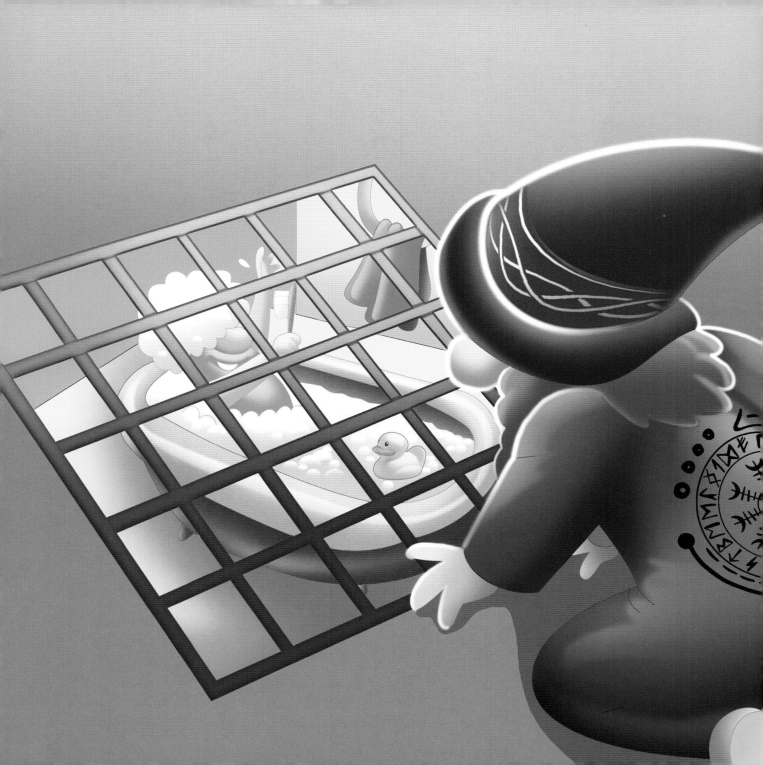

"Dad, I can't believe we've got to so many places using the Gonk transport network. Is there anywhere else we can go?"

"Of course there is Max. I think we should take a trip to the Tower of London. No rivers this time though.

Next stop, Westminster Station."

# "No WAAAAAYYYYY.

I can't believe there is an entire secret station beneath Westminster!" said Ruby.

"This station is special as it was not just built for passenger trains, but also for parcel trains. With so many letters being sent to the government, they need their own station to handle the post!"

*"Hop on folks, we're riding this mail train all the way to Tower of London!" said Alf.*

*"... this place is FULL of horrible history! For hundreds of years the Tower has been the home of some naughty (and some not so naughty) Gonks."*

*"Guy Fawkes, Sir Walter Raleigh and Anne Boleyn to name just a few."*

The family explored the Tower and saw the magnificent Crown Jewels.

The day was coming to an end and Alf,
Alma, Max and Ruby had seen some of
the most famous places in London.


"After all the dashing around today
I think our final journey can be a little
more peaceful" said Alf.

For other books and products from

please visit:

www.landofgonk.com

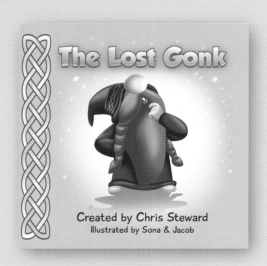

The Lost Gonk

Created by Chris Steward

Illustrated by Sona & Jacob